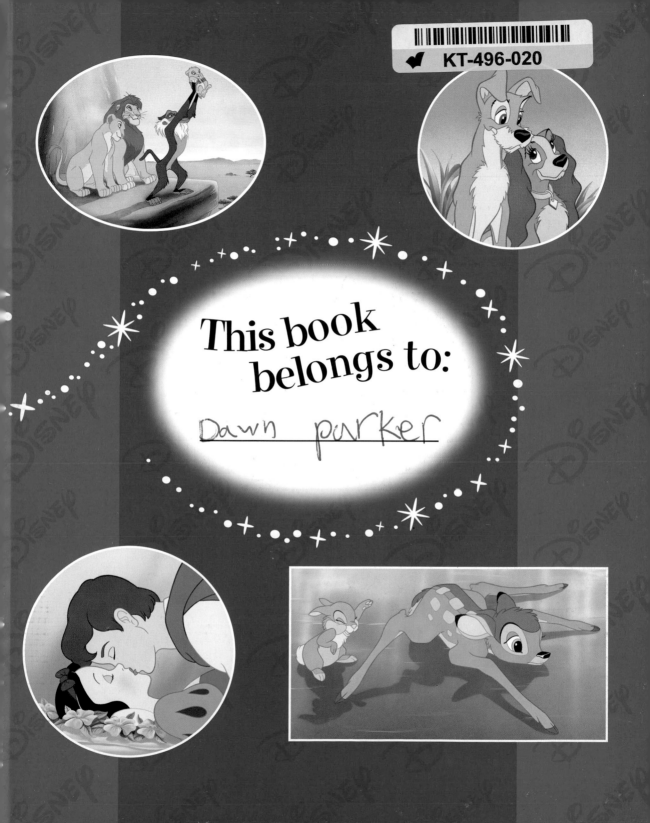

This book belongs to:

Dawn parker

CHICKEN LITTLE

FISH

BUCK CLUCK

STARRING

RUNT

ABBY

KIRBY

This is a Parragon book

First published in 2006

Parragon

Queen Street House

4 Queen Street

Bath, BA1 1HE, UK

ISBN 1-40546-184-5

Printed in China

p

It was nearly the end of the baseball game and it was down to Chicken Little, the smallest member of the team, to save the day for the team. As he slid towards home he was knocked sideways by the ball. The crowd groaned. Was Chicken Little out?

"Wait!" shouted the umpire, kicking a pile of dirt off Chicken Little. "The runner's safe!"

Chicken Little sighed with relief. He had won the game for the Acorns.

His year of shame was finally over.

A terrible year that had begun when he had brought widespread panic and destruction to Oakey Oaks by ringing the school bell and screaming that the sky was falling in. How was he to know that it was just a tiny acorn that had dropped on his head?

At long last, Chicken Little could put the whole sorry 'sky-falling incident' behind him. He was no longer the town joke. That nasty bully, Foxy Loxy had no reason to pick on him. And, best of all, his dad, Buck Cluck, was proud of him at last.

But Chicken Little's joy was to be short-lived. That very night he was standing in his bedroom admiring the stars when, **BANG**, a colourful panel fell on his head. And this time, it really was part of the sky!

Chicken Little knew he couldn't tell his dad, so he called over his trusty friends Abby, Runt and Fish.

"Talk to your dad," said Abby. But Chicken Little knew that his dad wouldn't listen.

The four pals stared at the panel. Strange wires and parts hung out of its back. Fish, who loved to fiddle, pressed a button and the panel began to shake. As it rose into the air, Fish jumped on to it. It zoomed around the room and...

...flew out of the window. Fish waved to his friends with his light stick, then disappeared into the night.

The three friends gave chase. They followed the beam of Fish's light stick until it came to a halt over the baseball field. They watched as an alien spaceship landed.

A door slid open and two aliens
floated out. They didn't see the
friends hiding in a dugout. But
Fish did. He waved to them from a
window of the spaceship.

Chicken Little knew that there
was only one way to save Fish.
They would have to board the
spaceship.

It was dark and spooky inside the ship. Chicken Little spotted a small
furry creature hanging in a blue light beam. It winked at Chicken Little and
he winked back. But Chicken Little couldn't stop. He hurried after his
friends. He didn't see the furry creature sprout legs and follow him.

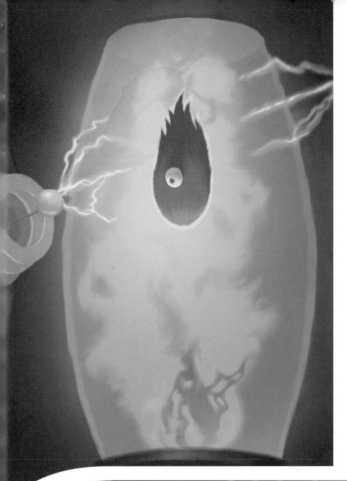

The friends soon found Fish. Then they found a strange map. It looked like some sort of battle plan. The aliens were taking over planets and Earth was next on their list. But before the friends could go for help, the aliens returned.

The aliens went straight to the blue light beam and saw that the furry
creature was missing. They seemed very upset. Then they saw Chicken
Little and his friends and chased after them.

The four friends tumbled out of the spaceship and hid in a cornfield.
In their rush to escape, they didn't notice the small furry creature
following them.

Suddenly, the alien's tentacles changed into blades and began slashing at the corn. The friends raced for the school. If they could just reach the bell they could warn the townsfolk that aliens were attacking!

As Chicken Little stood in front of the bell terrible memories
came flooding back. If he rung the bell everyone would think he
was crazy again. Foxy Loxy would start picking on him again,
making him the butt of the town's jokes. But Chicken Little
had to save the town. He yanked at the bell.

DiNG!
DONG!
DiNG!

As soon as he did, the aliens ran away. By the time Buck Cluck and
the rest of the town reached the school, the aliens and their spaceship had
completely vanished.

Nobody believed a word Chicken Little said.
"It's that acorn again," somebody moaned.
Even Buck Cluck thought his son was making things up.
Chicken Little was devastated.

Nobody noticed the small furry creature hiding nearby. If they had, they might have realised that he was a tiny alien child. He watched as the spaceship streaked across the night sky. His parents had left without him. He was sad and all alone. Then he spotted a friendly face – Chicken Little. He decided to follow him home.

The next day everyone was mad with Chicken Little. He was the town joke once more and his dad was more ashamed of him than ever.

Chicken Little sent his friends away and slunk off to be alone. Suddenly, the small furry creature crept out from the bushes. Chicken Little screamed. Abby, Runt and Fish raced back to see what was wrong.

When Fish heard the furry creature's gibberish, he understood exactly what he was saying. He explained to his friends that the little alien's name was Kirby and he wanted to get home to his parents. But before they could do anything something scary began to happen.

The sky began to rumble and crack. Buck Cluck and the rest of the town rushed outside to see what was happening.

The aliens were attacking Oakey Oaks. Kirby began to chatter excitedly. His parents were coming to get him.

The townsfolk began to panic. As they raced around, Kirby got caught up with them.

Chicken Little raced after his new friend. As a truck hurtled towards the tiny creature, Chicken Little jumped onto a car, bent back the aerial, and catapulted himself through the air. He grabbed Kirby and crashed right into the town's movie theatre.

"Chicken Little," cried Buck Cluck, grabbing his son's hand. He didn't see Kirby hiding behind the stage curtain.

Suddenly Abby appeared. "Deal with the problem," she shouted, meaning the chaos outside.

But the big rooster gave his tiny son a hug and apologized.

"You need to know I love you, no matter what," he said.

"I'm sorry if I ever made you feel like that was something you had to earn."

It was all Chicken Little had ever wanted to hear but this was no time to get soppy.

"Okay, Dad, now all we have to do is return this helpless kid," he explained, pulling the furry ball out from behind the curtain.

Kirby bared his teeth.

"Are you crazy?" began Buck. Then he stopped himself and began again. "Wonderful idea. Just tell me what you need."

Outside, aliens were zapping cars and townsfolk, making them disappear. Foxy Loxy had been one of the first to vanish.

Carrying Kirby, Buck followed his son up onto the roof of the town hall. But before they could hand back the furry child, they were trapped in a dark beam. Kirby was released and an angry voice boomed,

"YOU HAVE VIOLATED INTERGALACTIC LAW 902.4!"

Kirby began to babble excitedly. Slowly it dawned on the aliens that it had all been a huge mistake.

Buck and Chicken Little were freed. The aliens quickly returned all the townsfolk to normal – all except for Foxy Loxy, who was returned much sweeter and nicer than before.

"Sorry for all the trouble," apologised Tina, Kirby's mother. Then she went on to explain how they visited Oakey Oaks each year to collect the best acorns in the entire galaxy.

As the aliens boarded the spaceship, a panel fell off – the very same panel that had fallen on Chicken Little's head almost exactly a year before. The sky really had fallen on Chicken Little's head – not once but twice!

Oakey Oaks was so proud of Chicken Little that they made a film all about him. But no one was quite as proud of the tiny chicken as his dad, Buck Cluck!